Mr. Bear's Boat

THOMAS GRAHAM

E. P. Dutton • New York

Copyright © 1988
by Thomas Graham

All rights reserved.

Published in the United States
by E. P. Dutton,
2 Park Avenue, New York, N.Y. 10016,
a division of NAL Penguin Inc.

Published simultaneously in Canada by
Fitzhenry & Whiteside Limited, Toronto

Printed in Hong Kong
by South China Printing Co.
First Edition   W
10 9 8 7 6 5 4 3 2 1

Library of Congress
Cataloging-in-Publication Data

Graham, Thomas, date   Mr. Bear's boat
   Summary: Mr. Bear builds a sailboat
and takes Mrs. Bear for what they hope
will be a peaceful ride—but isn't.
   [1. Sailboats—Fiction.   2. Bears—Fiction]
I. Title.
PZ7.G7579Mo   1988   [E]   87-24466
ISBN 0-525-44375-4

11.95

89B452

HOW TO
MAKE A
SAILBOAT

Mr. BEAR
BAYVILLE
USA

for Louise & Ed
and Annie & Vinnie

Mr. Bear wanted to build a sailboat. He read a
book that told him how, and then he set to work.
    Nothing can beat the peace and quiet of sailing on
a hot summer day, he thought as he sawed, glued,
and sanded.

In the evenings, while Mr. Bear studied the book, Mrs. Bear cut the sails and hemmed their edges. "I can't wait to go sailing and have a nice picnic lunch," she said.

"A sailboat is a lot of work," said Mr. Bear. "We'll just have to wait a little while."

Every day Mr. Bear made progress. He attached the keel to the back, and the ribs to the keel.

"Will it be done soon?" asked Mrs. Bear as the boat began to take shape.

"It will be ready by the first hot day," answered Mr. Bear. "We'll just have to wait a little while."

It's hard to wait for something you really want, thought Mrs. Bear.

Mr. Bear screwed the planking to the ribs to make the bottom and the sides.

He fit the deck to the bow.

He slipped the tiller onto the fin-shaped rudder. He would use this to steer the boat.

He planed the mast.
It would hold the sails.

Now it really looked like a boat.
"Is it ready yet?" asked Mrs. Bear.
"Almost," said Mr. Bear. "The seats go in next."

When the seats were in, they hoisted the mast.

Mr. Bear hooked up the rigging, and Mrs. Bear
fastened the sails. A coat of varnish, and the boat
was done.

On the first hot day, they packed a picnic
lunch and took the boat to a nearby cove.
One good shove and they were off.

Mr. Bear kept his back to the wind and
his hand on the tiller. The sails swelled
and the boat sped out to the bay.

"Oh, this is fun!" exclaimed Mrs. Bear.
"So fast, and so peaceful . Just the two of us."
Until…

ROAARR

WHOOOSH

SPLAASH

"EEEK!" cried Mrs. Bear.

Then the wind died. And the tide went out. And
Mrs. Bear discovered the picnic basket was missing.
"Our lunch," she moaned.

Mr. Bear was grumpy, hot, and hungry. "This is not what I had in mind," he complained.

"I guess we'll just have to wait a little while," said Mrs. Bear.

She was right. In a little
while the wind came up,

the tide turned,

and Mrs. Bear spotted the picnic basket.
"Oh, boy!" said Mr. Bear.

Quickly, before the wind could die down again,
they sailed back to their own little cove,

where they tied up their boat, spread out their
picnic lunch, and didn't have to wait any longer.